MONSTER ROLLING SKULL AND OTHER NATIVE AMERICAN TALES

MONSTER ROLLING SKULL AND OTHER NATIVE AMERICAN TALES

RETOLD BY

ANITA GUSTAFSON

Illustrated by John Stadler

THOMAS Y. CROWELL NEW YORK

For Moppet,
who is as old and clever as Coyote
A.G.

To my friends
David Marshall and Michael Sheldon
J.S.

Printed in the United States of America.

Designed by Ellen Weiss

Library of Congress Cataloging in Publication Data
Gustafson, Anita.
Monster rolling skull and other native American tales.
SUMMARY: Retellings of nine traditional North American Indian tales.
1. Indians of North America–Legends. [1. Indians of North America–Legends] I. Stadler, John.
II. Title.
E98.F6G88 398.2′08997 79-7890
ISBN 0-690-04019-9
ISBN 0-690-04020-2 lib. bdg.

10 9 8 7 6 5 4 3 2 1
First Edition

CONTENTS

Coyote has been around for a long time. He's one of the Old Ones, the ones that came at the beginning, before the way of things was set. That's why he's part animal and part human.

Some say he's good. Some say he's bad. Some say he's wise. But some say he's only clever—too clever.

The truth of the matter is this: Coyote is sometimes one way and sometimes another, and sometimes all ways all jumbled together . . . because Coyote is one of the Old Ones.

MONSTER ROLLING SKULL

One day Coyote was strolling on the plains, and the sun was on his red-gold fur, and he was feeling warm and drowsy. He came to a tall cottonwood tree.

"I'll sleep in the shade of this tree," Coyote thought. He lay down, with a stone pillowing his head and another stone at his feet.

"If you guard me while I sleep," he said to the tree, "I'll reward you."

"Reward?" said the tree. "I'll do it!"

"This is the life!" Coyote sighed. He slept.

"How should I guard him?" the tree wondered. "I can't chase danger away. How fast can a tree run? And I can't shout loud enough to scare off a bluejay. I have to be careful. I've heard Coyote is tricky." The tree rustled and fretted. "There must be something I can do. I wish I were smart—like Coyote!"

An idea struck the tree. "But, of course! I know what to do! I am as smart as Coyote."

The tree took a deep breath and did what it knew it could do. It grew! A root shot out past Coyote's tail. Another shot past his head. A new trunk sprang up from the tips of the new roots. The tree grew and grew until only a few small openings remained just above Coyote's bed.

"Nothing can touch Coyote now!" The cottonwood sighed with relief, and its leaves danced in the sun. "I wonder what my reward will be?"

Soon Coyote woke up. It was almost dark in the tree. He couldn't get out.

"Tree!" Coyote called. *"Tree!"* Coyote shouted.

"You see who your friends are, Coyote!" The tree was proud. "I gave a whole year's

growth to guard you! You'll be safe in there all year."

Coyote squeaked.

"You bet!" the tree went on. "I won't be able to do another thing this year, but that's all right. The important thing is that you are safe. Where's my reward?"

"Let me out," said Coyote, "and I'll get it."

"I can't," said the tree, "but I want my reward."

"I can't get your reward until you let me out," said Coyote.

"Try to do a favor for someone and see what happens!" said the tree. "They told me you were tricky, Coyote!"

"Don't be dumb—"

"Dumb? Me?" interrupted the tree. "I am smart."

"Too smart," snapped Coyote. "And too smart is dumb. You outsmarted yourself."

"Very well, Coyote. Get yourself out!" The tree was angry now.

"Very well," Coyote said. "I will!"

"Hmmmpf!" said the tree.

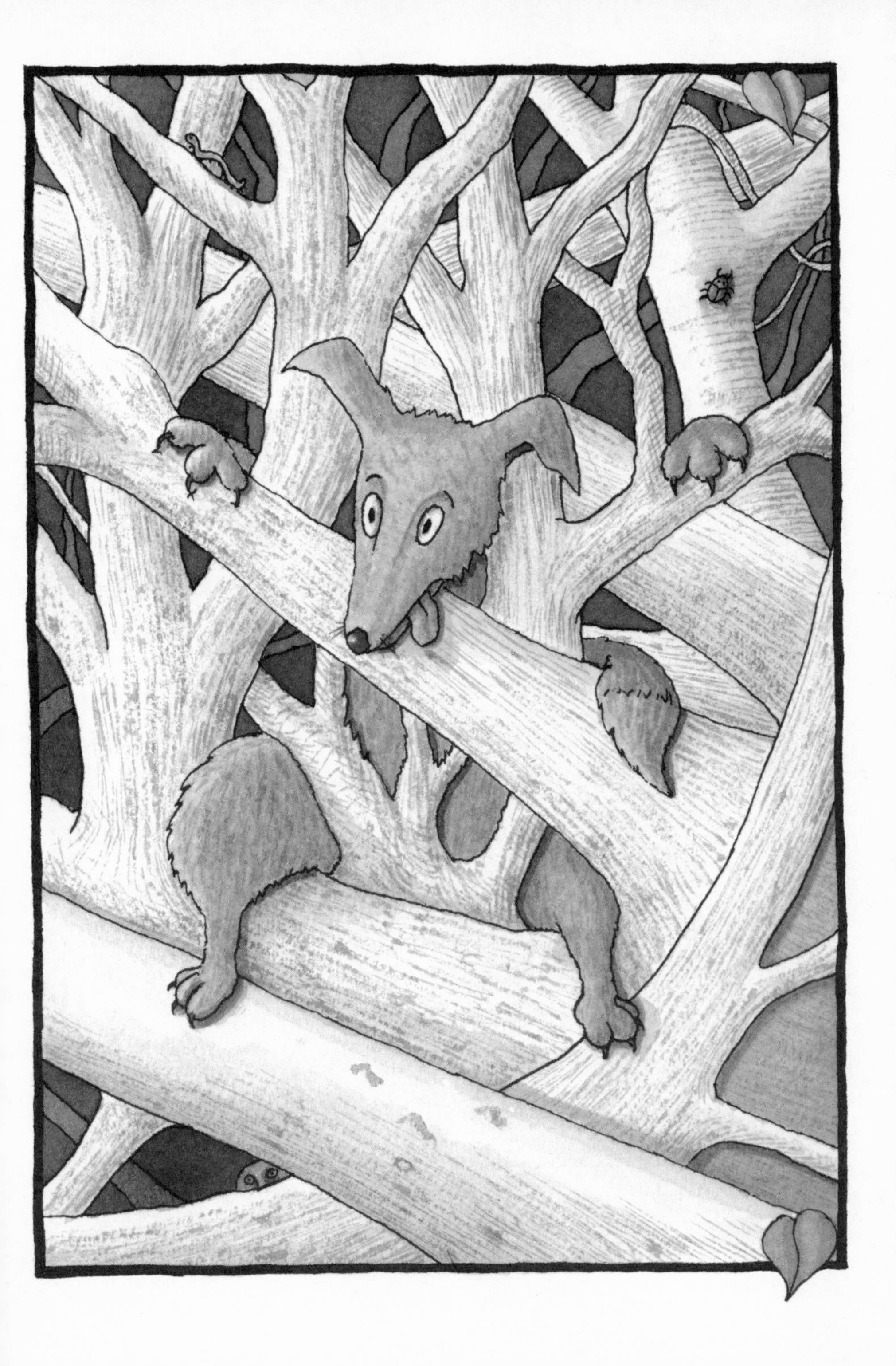

Coyote could see the grassy plains through the openings between the branches. He squeezed his head out, but his shoulders stuck. "That won't work," Coyote muttered. He squeezed his legs out, but his body stuck. "And that won't work."

Coyote sat on his stone pillow. After a minute, he said, "But *that* might work!" And he took one of the stones, laid his tail on the other. He pounded and pounded until his tail came off. He tossed his tail out of the tree and onto the ground.

"This will work! Already my tail is free."

Coyote laid one leg on the stone. He pounded and pounded until that leg came off.

"There!" said Coyote. He tossed that leg out. But when he backed into the opening, he saw that the other leg would have to come off. So he pounded and pounded and threw the other leg out. "That takes care of that!"

But now his arms stuck. Coyote pounded and pounded one arm off and threw it out. Now when he backed into the hole, his back part was free, but his arm and head were still trapped inside. And now, Coyote got *mad!*

"All right then," he muttered.

He snatched one stone, laid his head on the other, and pounded and pounded and *pounded* on his neck until his head came off.

"There!" he shouted as his body fell free onto the plains, and his head dropped inside the tree. *"I did it!"*

Coyote is one of the Old Ones, and Coyote has much power. It was easy for him to bounce his head through the hole. It was easy for him to bounce his head on the plains. It was easy for him to laugh.

"I am clever," Coyote laughed. "I am the most clever one in all the world! Tee, hee, hee! I am free!"

Coyote was so happy he rolled his head around on the ground. He went on rolling it along until he came to the top of a hill. A village lay below him, a circle of dwellings on the wide sunlit plains. In front of every dwelling was a cooking fire. On every fire was a pot.

"I'm hungry," Coyote said. "I'm always hungry. And there's food down there!"

Coyote rolled his head down to the village.

"Some kind of monster, that is!" said the people as they saw the rolling skull.

Coyote stopped rolling his head in the center of the village. He howled in a hollow voice:

"I am Monster Rolling Skull!"

"Quick! Throw a pot over it!" said the chief. The young braves did, but Coyote bounced his head and threw off the pot.

"Some kind of *strong* monster, that is!" said the people.

"A monster like that—do as he says!" said the chief.

"Bring me food! I want food!" Coyote howled in his hollow voice. "Put some food into this monster's pot!"

"A monster like that—he could eat us if we don't bring food!"

"I'll eat you if you don't bring food!" howled Coyote. "I am Monster Rolling Skull."

The people rushed to their dwellings. One found buffalo fat; another, parched corn; an-

other, deer meat; and another, wild parsnips. Whatever they had, the people brought and put into the monster's pot. Then they rushed back to their dwellings. At each one, a lookout was posted to make sure that Monster Rolling Skull did not come along to eat them up.

"Hee, hee, hee!" giggled Coyote. "I am so clever! Now I'll pull myself together and have a feast!"

So one after another after another, till all the lookouts in all the dwellings in all the village had seen, they all saw this:

Monster Rolling Skull rolling *out* of the village and over the hill and up to a cottonwood tree. They saw the monster roll to a stop by its body and its arm and pop itself onto them, then drag itself to its other arm and pop onto that, then crawl to where one leg was lying and pop together with that, then hop back to the other leg and pop together with that, then scamper back to the long bushy tail and pop that on, and then leap and laugh and sing this song: "Ha, ha, ha, ha, ha! I am smart and people are dumb!"

“Smart isn’t everything,” the tree said. “Take it from me.”

“Ha, ha, ha, ha, ha!” The monster leapt and laughed even louder.

“You can be *too* smart,” the tree said sadly, as the lookouts crept away to report to the village.

“Ha, ha, ha, ha, ha!” laughed Coyote. He ran back to the village to get the food in his monster pot. “Watch out for me! I am Monster Rolling Skull!”

“Ha, ha, ha, ha, ha!” laughed the people. “You are no monster. You are just Coyote, and you are just tricky! And this time, Coyote, you are *too—*”

Coyote stopped their words with a sad hungry howl. The people had taken all their food back! Nothing was left in Monster Rolling Skull’s pot!

Poor Coyote! How hungry he was! He crept off to beg for scraps.

HOW THE INDIANS GOT CORN

Coyote went on, growing more and more hungry. He came to a place where the people were harvesting. He saw their heavy baskets were rich with golden corn. He knew the people would feast that night. He hid and waited for the fires to be lit. When they were, he came from hiding and howled.

"Coyote is hungry," said the people. "Coyote is begging."

Coyote howled piteously.

"We have much! Coyote is welcome to share!"

Soon the fires burned low, and the night's darkness deepened. All the feast was eaten, and almost all the words had been said. One man turned to Coyote: "You were there in the beginning. . . ."

"That is true," Coyote nodded. "I was there in the beginning. I am one of the Old Ones."

"You are here now. . . ."

"This is true," Coyote agreed. "I am here now."

"You know many of the tales that have been made. . . ."

Coyote nodded. "I know *all* the tales."

"It would be fine to hear a tale now. . . ."

"Please tell us a story," begged a child.

Coyote nodded. The people had shared with him. He would tell them a tale.

"It was once told!" Coyote began.

A long time ago, only the Old Ones lived on earth. They were as Coyote is—part animal and part human. Then the first people were made. One man lived alone, far, far from any others.

He didn't know about fire. He ate only roots, bark, and nuts.

"I'm lonesome," he said one day. "And I'm tired of it. I'm tired of digging roots to eat. And gathering nuts. And stripping off bark. I'm tired of everything. I don't care if I eat or not."

So for days, he didn't dig roots, he didn't gather nuts, and he didn't strip bark. He slept.

While he slept, he dreamed. One day he awoke when it was nearly time for the sun to set. He saw someone standing quite near him.

"Who are you?" he asked. There was no answer.

"Come closer," he said, even though he was afraid.

"No." As the word was spoken, he saw a maiden. She was beautiful, with long, light hair.

"Very well," he said. "I will come to you."

"No." She turned and moved away.

"Wait!" he said.

She stopped and listened as he told her of his loneliness and of how tired he was of digging roots and gathering nuts and stripping bark. His words touched the maiden's heart.

"Do exactly as I tell you," she said when he had finished. "Promise this, and I will be with you always."

He promised, and she led him to a patch of dry grass.

"Get two dry sticks," she said. "Rub them together quickly, then hold them to the grass."

He did this, for he had promised to obey her words. Soon a spark flew out.

"I have never seen this!" the man said, alarmed.

"Do not worry. It is good," said the maiden.

The grass caught the spark, and as quick as that, the ground was burned over.

"This can't be good!" said the man.

"Do not worry. It is good," said the maiden. "When the sun sets, take me by the hair and drag me over the burned ground."

"I can't do that," he said, shaking his head.

"You must," she said. "You promised."

But still he would not agree until she explained.

"Wherever you drag me, something like

grass will spring up. You must care for this grass and give it water to drink. You must sing this song so it will grow strong."

She sang with a voice that was thin and liquid like water and yet full and rich like the soil of spring. Her song ran through his ears the way the moist spring soil ran through his fingers when he dug for roots. Her song was like something he knew, and he knew this song was good.

"The corn grows up [she sang].
The waters of the dark clouds drop, drop.
The rain descends.
The waters from the corn leaves drop, drop.
The rain descends.
The waters from the plant drop, drop.
The corn grows up.
The waters of the dark mists drop, drop."

"This I will do," said the man when he had learned the song. "But I don't like to drag you over the burned—"

She interrupted him with a look. "You promised," she said, and the man did not argue. The last of the sun disappeared from the earth. The maiden went on: "When you see between the leaves of the grass something like my long, light hair, then it is that you may use the seeds. Eat them, but save the biggest to plant again in the earth."

The sun was gone. In the darkness, a breeze sprang up, and the man heard the sound of the rustling of leaves. He lifted his hand to the maiden's head, then drew back in surprise. The maiden's hair had changed.

The man smiled, and there was joy in his heart, for now he knew that the maiden had come from the place where the spirits dwell. He did as he had promised. He dragged the maiden plant over the black-burned earth. He remembered the song and sang it. He knew what he did was good.

In the morning, he did not know if he had dreamed these things or if they had really happened. But as the grasslike corn sprang up, he saw that it did not matter. Whether the maiden was a dream or not, she had given him corn.

In the years that followed, the man con-

tinued to do as the maiden had said. And these things are still done to this day. When the people see the long, light hair silky on the cornstalk, they know that the beautiful Corn Maiden has not forgotten them and will never forget them or leave them. So all is well.

"So all is well," Coyote finished, and from around the moonlit fires came the murmurs of the people:

"So all is well. All is well. All is well."

THE SKELETON MAN

The grown-ups murmured around the fires. They were quiet and full and sleepy. But the children's eyes were wide-awake, as round as the moon above. Coyote smiled to see this.

"In the eastern forests," he began, "on nights when dogs weep at the death of autumn" —here he howled as a coyote does, a sobbing and spine-chilling howl—"a story is told of the dead who feast on the flesh of those who live."

"It was once told!" Coyote said, with a sharp, yipping sound.

A man and his wife left their village to hunt. When they had traveled for one day, they came to a clearing in the forest and stopped. They would build a sapling shelter and stay the night.

As they began to cut saplings, the man saw a lodge among the trees. No smoke or voice came from it, and the grass grew wild around it. "Look!" he shouted to his wife. "Someone has already built a lodge. Let us go in."

But the wife was suddenly afraid. "Think again, my husband," she said. "That lodge looks deserted, but perhaps there is sickness dwelling within."

"Bah!" said her husband. "It is almost night. Let us go in."

But still the wife was afraid. "Think again, my husband. Perhaps death lives within that lodge."

Clouds gathered and hid the last of the daylight. A rainwind sprang up. Thunder growled in the gloom.

"We will go in," said the husband. "I have decided."

Inside stood a bark box, one of those used to hold the bones of the dead.

"No one will bother us with talk," laughed the husband as he turned from it and looked around the lodge. "Tonight we'll sleep peacefully."

But the wife did not laugh. She stared into the box. A skeleton lay inside it, flat on its back, with its hands resting at its sides. The skull grinned up at her. Its jaw slowly yawned—but, no! That couldn't be! Surely her eyes were playing tricks on her! She turned away from the box.

"Let us build a fire," she said.

The husband went to gather wood. The woman took food from the pack—meat to broil and corn to pound and bake. *Click, Click.* She heard a sound like beads being strung. *Click, Click.* The sound seemed to come from the dead man's box. The woman whirled to look. The skeleton's hand was draped over the side of the box! The skeleton was alive—but, no! That couldn't be! Surely she only thought she had seen the skeleton's hands at its sides!

Her husband returned and built the fire.

Soon its crackle filled the lodge. Its light flickered on the walls. The cheerful sound and the dancing light soon eased the woman's fear.

"Sleep while I cook," she said, smiling at her husband.

He slept as she placed the meat to broil. He slept as she pounded the corn into meal. He slept as she shaped a corn loaf, placed it under the ashes to bake. That was when she heard a sound like someone chewing meat.

"My husband?" she whispered. No answer came. "My husband?" she spoke with a trembling voice.

But her husband was gone . . . *and the skeleton's hand no longer hung over the side of the box!* She saw dark red drops plopping to the earth under the skeleton's burial box!

A thin, hollow voice sighed from the box. "Is the bread nearly baked? I have had flesh; I must have bread." The voice sounded thin, as the wind sounds when it sighs through leafless trees. The woman froze in terror. "Is the bread nearly baked?" the voice sighed and died away. The woman could not answer.

The voice grew stronger. "Hurry the bread! Speed its baking!"

The woman heard the clicking sound, the sound of bone clicking on bone. The woman knew the skeleton man had eaten her husband's flesh and was gnawing on his bones.

"Hurry the bread! Speed its baking!" The skeleton's voice was sharp. "I must have bread! Then more warm and juicy flesh!"

With shaking hands, the woman piled wood on the fire to hurry the baking bread. All the while she piled the wood, the skeleton moaned from the box. The fire roared. Sparks flew up. The lodge was filled with heat. The woman had heard that spirits fear fire, but the skeleton man showed no fear.

"I must have bread!" he shrieked from his box.

The woman drew out the bread and threw it into the box. Bones clattered as the bread vanished.

"Now bring me flesh!" demanded the voice. "Bring me warm, juicy flesh!"

The woman tore a long strip of hickory bark

from the walls of the dead man's lodge. Frantically she twisted it and put one end in the fire. All the while she did this, she talked to the skeleton man.

"Here are my fingers, my sputtering broiled fingers. I burned them in the fire. They're not much use to me," she said, and she tossed a piece of the broiling meat into the skeleton's box.

Then, "What good is a hand without the fingers? Here is the rest of my hand," and she tossed more broiled meat into the box.

She saw that the torch of hickory bark was kindled in the fire.

"What good is an arm without a hand? While you eat my arm, I'll get you water," and she tossed the last of the meat into the box. She snatched up the torch and ran out into the stormy night.

Swiftly she ran, lighting her way with the torch. But halfway home she heard a sound.

Click, Click!

The skeleton man pursued her! Lightning slashed and thunder cracked. *Click, Click!* On and on, she ran. The dead man gained on her. *Click,*

Click! She heard his angry shriek, his cry of hungry fury: *"I want warm and juicy flesh!"*

The rain pelted down. The ground grew slick. The woman stumbled and fell, and the skeleton man drew nearer. She felt his breath upon her neck—but there! Her village was just ahead.

She scrambled up and ran again, ran to save her life. She felt his hand touch her shoulder—but there! The lodge of her family. She fell through the door flap and into the lodge. She was safe!

Outside, a shriek rang through the forest. Thunder rolled and clapped, and then the skeleton man . . . had vanished!

She was safe in her family's lodge.

The village gathered to hear her tale.

"Ay-ah," said the old chief. "In the days when my father was young, an evil wizard man lived. He boasted he would never die. I heard the story when I was young, and I thought it was only a story." The old man sadly sighed. "But the wizard did not boast. His are the bones you found. We must find a way to make him know he is dead."

A shaman was called, one with great medicine, one who was strong and good. She listened gravely and nodded her head. "I know what to do."

In the morning the sky was clear. The day would be fair and bright. Everyone went through the new-washed forest to the lodge of the skeleton man.

The medicine woman stepped forward, her face clear and calm. She entered the lodge, and came out again, carrying the wizard's bones. She threw them down and covered them with mud. She danced alone on the wizard's bones, until the mud was smooth and packed. She chanted a song which had never been heard by any who lived in the village.

And the shriek and whoop of the wizard man argued from under the mud. The people shrank to hear it. But the medicine woman smiled and gathered all her power. She spoke again her mighty words. The wizard man grew quieter. Once more she chanted and packed more mud on the bones of the wizard man. His shrieks faded into silence. The medicine woman raised her arms and threw her chant up to the skies. The birds burst into song.

And then it was that the people smiled. They entered the lodge without fear. They gathered the bones of their kin, their friend—the man who had died the night before. They buried him in the way they had seen, and sent his spirit to the Land of the Ghosts.

"Some say that bones under earth cannot rise and walk in the night," Coyote said. He rose and moved from the light. He couldn't be seen, but his voice came clearly. "But I who am Coyote, I who am clever—I am not so sure. For on nights when the autumn is dying, when dogs cry at the harvest moon"—Coyote howled in the wide-eyed night—"I have heard the sound of clicking, the sound of the walking dead. . . ."

"Bah!" said one man softly. "That is only a story."

Then came a sound like the clicking of beads, then the sound of panting laughter, and then Coyote . . . Coyote was gone.

THE WARRING HANDS

Coyote went on. He walked south for many days. Now he walked in bright sunshine.

"Travel!" he said. "That's what's needed at this time of year!"

"You're right," agreed Coyote's right arm.

"How else can I avoid shivering and freezing in the blizzards on the plains?" said Coyote.

"Or the cold rains of the northwest," agreed Coyote's right arm.

"Or the bitter, shaking cold of the northeast," Coyote continued.

"You couldn't," agreed Coyote's right arm.

"Who cares?" said Coyote's left arm. "This is boring!"

"What a rude thing to—" began Coyote's right arm, but Coyote interrupted.

"What's this?" he said. "Let us not quarrel. Let us all get along and work together and have a good time."

"Very well," said Coyote's right arm.

"I'm bored," said Coyote's left arm, and it sighed and fell asleep.

Coyote came to a land where flat-topped hills rose from flat sandy soil. He saw that the hills were high and steep-sided and that there were caves in the sides.

"What's this?" Coyote said. "I must go see what's in those caves!"

On the side of one mesa, Coyote found a series of small holes. Into these he put his hands and feet and crawled up to the caves. Halfway up, a tantalizing smell wandered aimlessly in the still air. The smell floated gently to Coyote's nose.

"What's this?" Coyote said. "I smell food!"

He was hungry, so he climbed faster. When

he came to the caves, he saw wide ledges in front of them. On these, he saw groups of women cooking in clay pots.

Ah! the smell was delicious! Coyote crept closer. He hid himself carefully. He schemed how to snatch a pot.

Soon he saw his chance. One woman stood and moved away from her pot. Coyote dashed to it, snatched it from the fire—so hungry he was that he didn't feel the heat—and ran off with the pot to a hiding place. He began eating with his right hand.

"Delicious!" he howled happily, his mouth full.

Suddenly his left hand grabbed the pot.

"What's this?" said the right arm. "Give me that pot back. It's mine!" The right arm hit the left arm. "Let go!" The left hand did. The right hand went back to dipping out food.

But soon the left hand grabbed the pot again. The right hand hit it. Snatch! Hit! It happened again and again. The pot went back and forth. Coyote ate from whichever hand had food in it.

But soon the quarrel became serious, because both hands were so busy snatching at the pot that they had stopped dipping up food to put in Coyote's mouth.

"Settle this quickly!" Coyote said sternly as the right arm claimed the pot. "I'm hungry!"

The right hand set the pot down immediately and dipped up food. But the left hand was so angry, it snatched the food from the other hand. The right hand snatched it back. Back and forth went the food. It was getting snatched into a pulp!

"I'm hungry!" howled Coyote. "Stop this!"

Now the right hand dipped another portion of food, and the left hand snatched that, and this went on until all the food in the pot was snatched into a pulp.

"Feed me!" howled Coyote.

But now the hands were so furious that they forgot the food and snatched at *each other.* The hands wrestled and tried to pinch and gouge each other. And between them was Coyote, watching them fight and still hungry.

The women came running to catch the thief.

And this is how they found Coyote—hands in a death grip above the pot of mashed food, and him howling how hungry he was.

"Oh, you Coyote!" said one, as she took back her pot.

"Wait!" howled Coyote, "I'm still hungry!"

"You've eaten your share," said the woman, looking at the food in the pot. "But look! Coyote has mashed my beans for me!"

"Sometimes," said an older woman, "Coyote does tricks that are good for the people when he *thinks* he's helping himself!"

The women laughed and went away.

And Coyote? There he sat with his hands locked together until the sun fell below the edge of the mesa. In the darkness, his hands, tired from fighting all day, fell apart. Coyote walked off in the dark to find the women and beg for food.

COYOTE FREES THE BUFFALO

Coyote went on. He walked north for many days. He came to a place where the Indians were in a council.

"You look serious," Coyote said.

"We are," said the chief. "We're so serious we don't have time for your tricks. Go away!"

But Coyote didn't want to go away. He saw that the people looked more winter hungry than usual. So he remained where he was and said: "You yourself have said I'm a schemer. Tell me your trouble. Perhaps I can scheme a way to help you."

Nothing else had worked, the people said to themselves and to each other. This great schemer, this Coyote, might be able to help.

"Here is our trouble," the chief began. "Soon spring will come. Already one can smell spring in the air of winter."

"That's your problem?" said Coyote.

"Don't interrupt," said the chief.

"Very well," said Coyote.

"Every spring, the Spirit Master in the south opens the caves from which the buffalo come. The great herds travel north in summer, eating and growing fat. Thus it is that they come, and thus it is that we have meat to eat, and skins to cover us and make homes, and bones for tools and weapons. The buffalo, as you know, is our brother. He is happy to die for us, his little brothers. This is the way of things, and this is good. But this year . . ." The chief broke off and shook his head.

"This year," said Coyote, "it's *not* the way of things?"

"This year," said the chief, "all the buffalo are trapped in the mountains by an old man who

lives there with his young cousin. This man had great power once. Long ago he owned all the buffalo. But the animals helped the buffalo escape one by one. Now the old man has taken the buffalo back, and he won't free them. What will happen to us?"

Coyote thought for only a second before he knew a scheme to help these people.

"It's simple," he said. "You want a way to free the buffalo—that's all."

"We know *that,*" said the chief. "But we can't think how to do it—*that's* the problem."

"Simple," said Coyote. "Here's what you do. In three days' time, get on your horses and ride out. You'll see the buffalo roaming free on the plains. Leave the rest to me!"

"Very well," said the chief and all the people.

Coyote left. He walked along and found a prairie dog. "Go and wait by the well where the young cousin draws water for the old man. The child will take you home for a pet. Slip off in the night and—" Coyote whispered the rest of his scheme to the prairie dog.

"Very well," said the prairie dog when it had heard all the plan.

The prairie dog went to the well, and the young cousin came to draw water. He saw the prairie dog and greeted it, but he did not take it home for a pet. The prairie dog returned to tell Coyote this.

"One day has passed for nothing then," said Coyote. "But we'll try again."

This time Coyote sent the killdee.

The child came and found the killdee. He liked it very much and took it home.

"Look here!" he said to the old man. "This bird of mine is very good."

"Good for nothing!" snapped the old man. "There is nothing living on the earth that isn't a rascal or a schemer. Take it back where you found it."

The child didn't like to do this, but he obeyed.

"Two days have passed for nothing," said Coyote, when the killdee came back to him. "But we'll try again."

This time Coyote sent a dainty red fox.

"Look here!" said the child to the old man. "This is a nice pet to have."

"You are foolish," said the old man. "That one, too, is good for nothing. All the animals in the world are schemers. I'll kill this one with a club."

The child took the fox in his arms and cried, "No! This animal is too small! If you kill this animal, I'll run away!"

"Very well," said the old man. "You are foolish, but keep it if you must. I have lost much in my life. I do not wish to lose you."

The child clutched the fox, cuddled it, and smiled.

When the fox did not return by nightfall, Coyote was pleased and said, "All is well. The buffalo will be freed by the third morning as I promised."

During the night, the fox remembered Coyote's instructions and slipped from the child's arms. It stole to the pen of the trapped buffalo, slipped through the fence, and ran among them, barking and squalling. The buffalo were terrified. They milled around in the pen, then ran toward the gate, piling up on each other in their fear. They broke the gate as they thundered toward the plains. The old man heard the noise.

"Where is your pet?" he asked, shaking the child awake.

"It is gone," said the child.

"I told you so!" shouted the old man. "Now you see that animals are bad. Now our buffalo have escaped again, and now you'll be hungry!"

The old man ran to the door and shouted after the fleeing buffalo: *"Go! You're as bad as every other creature on the face of the earth!"*

The next morning the people came on the backs of their horses. They looked out and saw the plains were darkened with vast herds of buffalo. They saw that the number of buffalo was uncountable, and their hearts were glad. The buffalo were back, and this was the way of things, and this was good. There would be much of everything they needed.

And, yes, there would be much to share with those who couldn't hunt, for sharing, too, was the way of things and sharing, too, was good.

No one would be hungry, not even the old man and the child.

"Coyote's tricks have helped us this time," said the people. "Coyote is a great schemer, and Coyote can do much good for the people when Coyote wishes!"

And the smell of spring was sharp and pungent in Coyote's nose, and the words of the people were warm in his ears. And Coyote's heart was glad.

THE MAIDEN'S PROMISE

The people had feasted, and now they sat around the fires.

"It was once told!" Coyote said. A hush fell, and the people listened to his story.

The people (Coyote said) were living together in a large camp. Their chief had a beautiful daughter.

"Do you not think it is time for you to marry?" the chief asked his daughter one day. "You have refused all the men in this camp, but you need someone to hunt while you take care of things at home."

"It is true what you say, Father," said the daughter.

"Good!" said the father.

"But," continued the daughter, "I have my own fine skin house, so I do not need a husband for that."

"As do all the women," agreed the father.

"And I have my own garden and my name, which I own and will pass on to my children, so I do not need a husband for that."

"As do all the women," agreed the father.

"And for what I *do* need, I do not wish it from any of the men here!" said the daughter.

"And what is it that you *do* need?" The father was growing short-tempered.

"I need one who can share life with joy," said the daughter slowly, thinking deeply. "And that is what I wish."

"That's a fine wish," said the father, "but it's time for you to choose and marry one who will hunt for you, and that's that!"

"Very well," said the daughter. "If I need a hunter, here's how I will choose. There must be two contests, one for shooting and one for

trapping. The one I will marry must win *both* contests."

"Good!" said the father. "Do you promise that?"

"Father!"

"Of course you do. I'm sorry. Your word in a promise has never been broken," said the father.

"And never will be," added the daughter.

It happened that Sun and Star, who were brother and sister, were listening. They decided to test this beautiful maiden's promise.

During the darkness they erected a lodge on the outskirts of the camp. The poles were old and badly chosen. The covering was tattered and patched, made of old, cracked tule mats. The floor was strewn with coarse dried brush and grass, and the beds were heaps of this coarse stuff. Their blankets were ragged; their kettles and cups were made poorly of bark. Star took on the form of an old woman in rags. Sun was a dirty boy with sore eyes.

In the morning, the people of the camp gossiped with each other about the newcomers and how poor they seemed.

Then the chief's speaker came. He announced the two marriage contests.

"Tomorrow morning an eagle will land in that tall tree. Everyone will have two shots. Whoever kills the eagle will win that contest. Tomorrow night traps will be set high in the mountains. Whoever can trap two fine, furry fishers—one light and one dark—by the next morning will win that contest. Whoever can win *both* contests will have the Chief's daughter in marriage."

"Does she promise?" asked one young man.

"Don't be silly!" snapped the chief's speaker.

"I'm sorry," said the young man. "Of course she does."

Each young man thought eagerly of how on the next day he would shoot the eagle. But the next morning, as they shot their arrows, one after another missed.

"There will be no winner," said the father as he watched with his daughter. The daughter smiled.

Suddenly the old ragged woman came from her tattered lodge, raised her arm to gain attention, and pulled back the entrance flap.

Whiz!

An arrow shot from inside the lodge. It soared to the top of the tall tree, and the eagle fell to the ground.

"The poor boy in that poor lodge has won this contest!" said the astonished father.

The old woman cackled and croaked, "Come here, daughter!"

The daughter walked to the poor lodge. The old woman held the flap aside and said, "Do not enter. He is sick. But you can take a long look at the winner of this contest!"

The poor maiden! There on the bed lay the filthy boy with sore eyes. Even from where she stood, the smell of sickness reached her.

"You promised!" cackled the old woman.

"I did," replied the beautiful maiden, tears springing to her eyes. "And I keep my promises."

Through the rest of that day, the young men of the camp carefully set their traps to do what

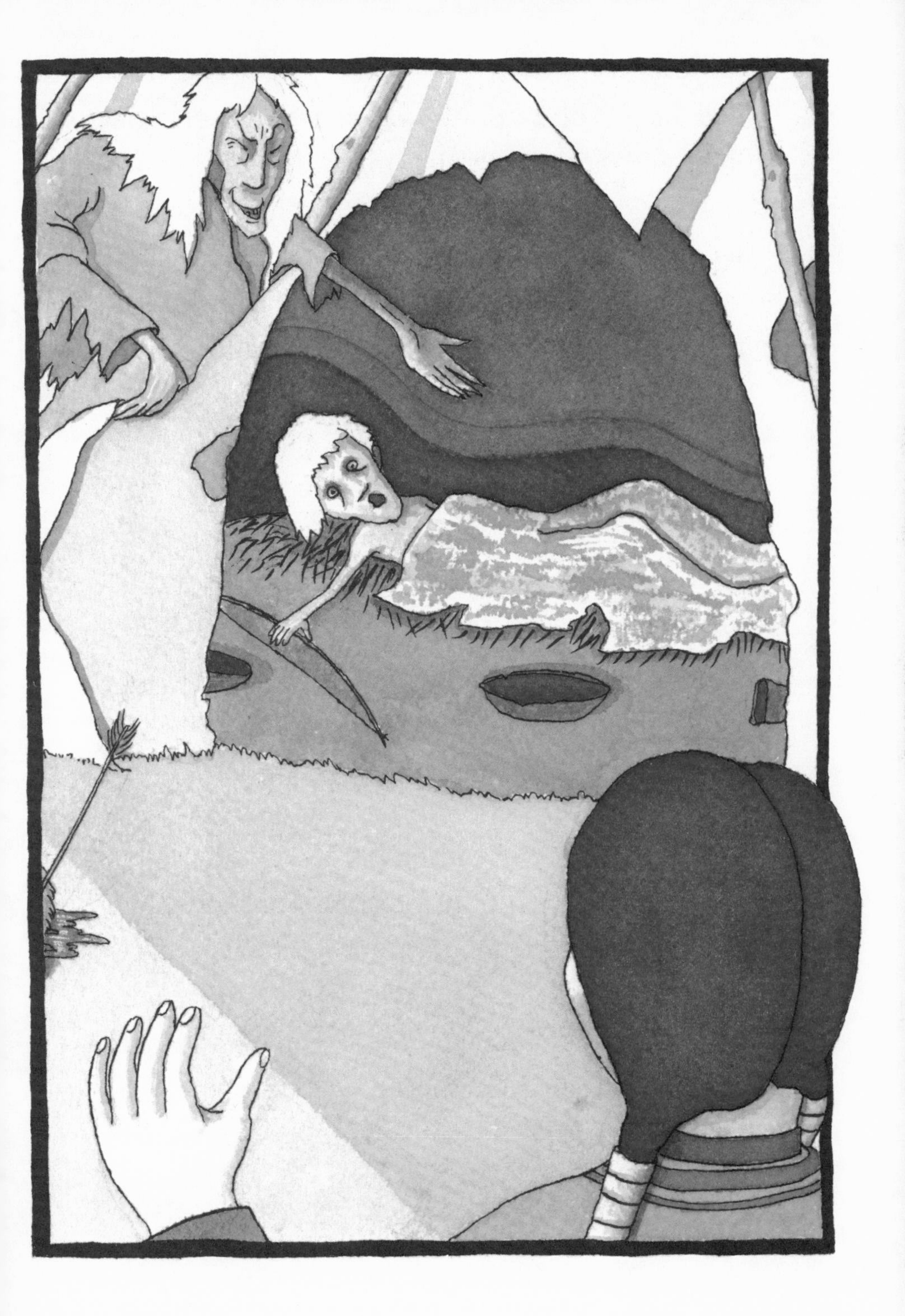

had never been done—catch two fishers, one light and one dark. That night, the old woman and the dirty boy hobbled and coughed as they set their traps out. They didn't bother to climb high in the mountains as the young men had. Instead they set their traps on the edge of the camp, a place where *no* fisher had ever been caught.

In the morning, the young men checked their traps. There were no winners.

"At least," thought the father as he inspected the traps, "that sick boy won't catch anything with traps set on the edge of the camp."

But as he returned from the mountains, the old woman came out of her tattered lodge, raised her arm to gain attention and croaked, "Now look here at my grandson's traps!"

She held two traps high. In one was a dark fisher, and in the other was a light fisher. Both were fully as big as a fox, with perfect, furry tails.

"Your daughter must marry my grandson!"

The father's heart sank. "He is sick," he argued with the old woman. "He will not live long."

"Long enough to marry!"

"Very well," he sighed. "I will tell her."

"Very well," the maiden sighed when she had heard. "I have promised, and it must be done."

She went to the lodge, and the old woman emerged.

"Go away!" croaked the old woman. "My grandson doesn't want to bother with you today. Come back tomorrow."

The maiden returned to her father's lodge, through the dust and the pity of the camp. Some murmured that she shouldn't have to marry this mean and dirty boy. To them, she said: "I promised."

For three days, matters remained this way, and the murmurs of the people grew louder. On the evening of the third day, Sun said to his sister, "We will take our true forms tonight."

During the darkness, the old mat lodge became a fine new skin lodge, richly decorated with ornaments and paint, with streamers tied to the top. The old bark kettle became a bright copper kettle, filled with a shimmering liquid. In the

lodge were new woven baskets and embroidered and painted bags. The old woman became as she truly was—a tall handsome woman, her clothes shining with twinkling lights. The dirty boy became as he truly was—young and handsome, his long hair shining like the rays of the sun, his clothes covered with shining copper.

In the morning, the people of the camp gossiped to each other that a rich chief had come and thrown the poor people out. They were glad, for they thought this meant the promise wouldn't have to be kept.

But the maiden said, "I promised. I must find where my husband has gone. I will ask at the rich lodge."

As the maiden drew near to the lodge, Star emerged gracefully. "Come, meet your husband," she said warmly. The maiden was startled.

Sun emerged and took the maiden to stand with him by the copper kettle. He lifted it and poured the shimmering liquid over the maiden. Lines of tiny sparkling stars formed on her. The

liquid ran on the ground, made a path of gold dust to the chief's lodge.

"This will be your trail when you visit your people," Sun said to his new wife.

Seeing this, the chief and the people knew who the strangers were. Now they rejoiced. The wedding feast was long and happy.

In the years that followed, each visit of Sun and his wife were occasions for more feasts, so happy were the people to see them and to share their happiness. Promises were made "by the maiden's promise" during these times. Such promises were kept, and the people grew stronger and happier through the strength of the kept promises.

"And so it is even today, that the gathering of the people to celebrate special joys strengthens and makes happy those who gather," Coyote said. He raised his front legs, and waved his tail, and howled at the moon from happiness. And the people smiled.

THE MEDICINE OF BLOODY HAND

"Tell us another," the people begged.

Coyote thought of a tale he had heard in the eastern forests. "It was once told!"

Bloody Hand was a great hunter. Never did he leave his lodge to hunt but he found much game. Never did he aim his arrow but it found the mark. And never did he take life without leaving behind meat for the remaining animals to eat.

One day Bloody Hand hunted with a party of other men. Enemy warriors fell upon them.

Bloody Hand was wounded and left to die on the floor of the forest.

Then it was that the animals came, and the birds flew down, and the insects crawled, and all things came to mourn him.

Spider wept and began to weave. A spider's web is one good way to staunch the flow of blood. But Bloody Hand was dead, and Spider could not help him.

And Spider wept so piteously that a bird came from its perch and spoke: "Do not cry."

But Spider wept.

"Do not sorrow."

But Spider wept.

"Do not mourn, do not mourn. The birds will bring Bloody Hand back to life!"

The animals agreed that this was a good thing to do. They left the birds to discuss the best way to do it. Only Spider remained.

The Council of Birds sent Crow to fly swiftly and strongly in the air, to flap above the wisps of the clouds and the winds of the earth, to the Spirit Bird who from the beginning has dwelt there.

"Caw!" called Crow. "Caw! O Spirit Bird, we need your help. We wish to bring Bloody Hand back to life."

"You and who else?" the Spirit Bird snapped. He hated to have his naps disturbed.

"All the birds," said Crow. "The council of birds has sent me."

"Eagles, too?" The Spirit Bird looked suspicious.

"Yes, Father, even the eagles."

"Good!" The Spirit Bird nodded to himself. "Eagles are pushy, you know," he explained to Crow.

"Please, Father," said Crow, "Bloody Hand lies dead on the floor of the forest. We wish to bring him back to life."

"Simple, simple," muttered the Spirit Bird. "Well, you have my permission. Go ahead." The Spirit Bird yawned.

"But we don't know what to do!"

"Well, why didn't you say so!"

"Father, I—"

"Here's what you do," the Spirit Bird interrupted. "Have each bird make this sacred

sound"—here the Spirit Bird made the sound— "Then they must sing this song of great power." (Here the Spirit Bird sang the song.) "A stalk of a plant, light green and tender, will spring from the ground. That's the small-dose plant, and—"

"That's what?" asked Crow.

"Small dose. That's what you call it and that's what you give," said the Spirit Bird, with a look that warned against further interruption. "Keep singing that song, and the stalk will grow. Keep singing, and the stalk's veins will run with blood. Keep singing, and snap the stalk. Catch the blood and—remember, you have to keep singing!—mix it with the seed of a squash and—sing, sing, sing—give this medicine to . . . ah. . . ." The Spirit Bird waved his wing.

"Bloody Hand," Crow said.

"Right," the Spirit Bird said. "Then you sing and you sing and you sing, and soon he will come to life."

"Thank you, O Spirit Bird."

"It's nothing," said the Spirit Bird.

"I will leave you and return to—"

"Wait!" said the Spirit Bird. "Who is this . . . ah. . . ."

"Bloody Hand," said Crow.

"Right," the Spirit Bird said. "Some kind of hawk?"

"He is human," said Crow.

"Oh." The Spirit Bird thought for a minute. "He have any tobacco?"

"Yes," said Crow.

"I haven't had a whiff of tobacco for . . . ah. . . ." The Spirit Bird waved his wing.

"A long time," said Crow.

"Right."

"You shall have some, Father."

"Good!"

Crow left him then, and through the wisps of the clouds, he returned to the winds of the earth. The Council of Birds did as they were told. They made the sacred sound. They learned the song and sang it as the powerful plant grew. They sang it as they mixed the plant's blood with the seed of the squash. When the medicine was made, Chickadee took a small dose, entered Bloody Hand's mouth, and spat it down his throat. And all the while, the Council of Birds sang the medicine song of their spirit father.

"Now, let it begin to work over all his body," they sang.

Slowly, slowly, the color returned to Bloody Hand's death-whitened face. Slowly, slowly, he awoke and heard the medicine song of the Council of Birds. Slowly, slowly, he came back to life, and Spider wept no more. Slowly, slowly, Bloody Hand began to learn the medicine song of the birds.

He sat, then stood. All things came to greet him, to welcome him back to the living.

Bloody Hand looked at the beauty of the forest. He thanked the birds. He talked with Crow.

"Just a whiff," said Crow.

Bloody Hand knelt and drew forth his tobacco. He made a small fire. The smoke rose in the air and lifted to the Spirit Bird high above the earth.

Bloody Hand returned to his people, and there was great joy. He taught his people how to heal in the way that he had been healed. He gave his people the powerful plant. He taught them why it was good to leave offerings after the hunt. All these things are medicine, he taught, and these are the things that give power.

Coyote stopped. There was a moment of silence. Then one of the people stood, carved a great chunk from a buffalo haunch, and carried it into the dark. Coyote was pleased. To give thanks gave the people power.

The feast was ended, and Coyote was full. Tomorrow he would go on.

THE FEAST THAT WASN'T

The next day Coyote went on. He was filled with good spirit, so when he saw Rattlesnake, he said, "Come to my house tomorrow."

"Of course," said the snake.

"We will feast together," Coyote said.

"Of course," said the snake.

That snake is not a big talker, Coyote thought, but he is welcome in my house.

The next morning the snake came to Coyote's house.

"Welcome!" said Coyote. "I have food. Enter, friend snake, and eat with me."

"Of course," said the snake, and he entered, slipping and gliding over the ground.

How quietly and quickly this snake moves! Coyote thought.

The snake coiled in a corner, and Coyote said, "I have cooked rabbit meat for you." As he put food in a bowl, Coyote could feel the snake's unblinking eyes watching him. How strongly this snake can stare! Coyote thought. He set the bowl in front of the snake.

"I will not eat this food," said the snake.

"It is good food, friend snake," said Coyote. "I have cooked it myself." To himself he thought that there was something strange about any creature that didn't like rabbit.

"I will not eat this *cooked* food," said the snake.

"What will you eat?" Coyote asked politely, but he didn't feel polite at all. He felt confused.

"Raw food," said the snake. "Healthy food. Corn pollen."

"I'll bring you some."

"Of course," said the snake. Coyote left to

find the pollen, and the snake thought: My ways are not the ways of this coyote, but I know he is trying hard to please me. This is good and in the nature of things. In this way we can truly become friends.

"Here is corn pollen," Coyote said when he returned. "Come, snake, and eat with me."

"Of course." But the snake didn't move to take it. Instead he said, "Put some on my head."

Coyote did as the snake asked. And the snake flicked his tongue the way the lightning flicks at the close of a hot summer day. With each flick, the snake licked pollen from the pile on top of his head. Coyote saw how fast the snake's tongue moved, and he began to grow nervous.

This snake is very different from me, Coyote thought, and this snake has power I don't. Aloud he said, "Will you eat more?"

"Of course." The snake shook his rattle to show his appreciation, but Coyote only grew more uneasy.

This snake is strange, thought Coyote, and I think it's best to do as he says. Again and again the snake flicked the pollen into his mouth, but never did the snake blink or move, and he did not speak or rattle again.

When the snake had finished, he abruptly uncoiled and glided toward the door, pausing to say, "Come to my house tomorrow. We will feast together."

"Of course!" Coyote said.

Now the snake was gone, and Coyote grew more and more fearful. The snake was so strange and so full of power. What would happen if he went to the snake's house? What should he expect?

Coyote dashed out to ask what to expect at the snake's house.

"Bats," said a deer. "Snakes eat bats."

"Rats," said a moose.

"I like rats—"

"Raw rats," said the moose.

Coyote gagged and went on. He asked a bear.

"Coyotes," said the bear.

"Coyotes!" squeaked Coyote.

"Raw coyotes," repeated the bear with an air of certain knowledge.

And now Coyote was frantic with fear. "What can I do? What can I do?" he muttered as he paced in his house. "That snake surely plans to eat *me!*"

Then a scheme came to him, and "That's it!" shouted Coyote, "I've got it!"

The next morning Coyote came to the snake's house. He was dirty, his fur covered with bits of leaves and pieces of grass and tiny balls of mud.

"My friend," said the snake as he welcomed Coyote, "you don't look well."

"I *feel* well!" said Coyote. "It's a fine morning for a glide on the ground. Yes, sir! A morning like this—makes you want to shake your rattle!" and Coyote wagged his tail.

The snake's eyes opened even wider. Coyote had filled a gourd with tiny pebbles and tied it to his tail. Aha! thought Coyote, seeing the snake stare, this scheme is working. Already that snake thinks I'm one of his kind. Now he won't think of eating me!

"Enter," said the snake, and Coyote slid in, not silently as the snake had done, but clawing and scratching on the ground and raising dust and making noise.

"I have food," the snake said. "I have cooked rabbit meat and cooked—"

Coyote interrupted him. "Good! Good! And you have pollen, I hope. I'm like you, you know. I like pollen. Give me some pollen."

Coyote curled in a corner of the snake's house. He forced his eyes not to blink. Soon his eyes grew red and watered. But the snake never blinked, so he wouldn't blink. Tears ran down Coyote's cheeks.

This coyote is acting strangely, thought the snake, but I'll give him pollen because he's my guest, and perhaps we'll become friends.

The snake placed a bowl of pollen before Coyote and took for himself a fresh raw rat.

"Put the pollen on my head," Coyote said to the snake, and the snake did. Coyote licked and licked, but as hard as he tried, his tongue couldn't reach the pollen piled on his head.

The snake watched Coyote struggle, growing more and more alarmed. Who knows what a coyote will do when a crazy spell comes on him? the snake thought.

"Eat with me, friend snake," said Coyote, thinking he would wipe the pollen from his head with his paw when the snake's head was turned. This he did, looking up just as the snake began to eat.

Coyote gasped. *The snake had unhinged its jaw!*

This was the biggest mouth Coyote had ever seen! He leapt to his feet and howled in fear.

Now the snake was shocked. He stared at Coyote, at the red weeping eyes and the mangy coat, at the long thin nose tensed in a howl.

Now Coyote stared at the unblinking snake, at the half-eaten rat dangling from the huge open mouth.

I am in danger, thought Coyote.

I am in danger, thought the snake.

Coyote edged away from the snake. The snake edged away from Coyote. For what seemed hours each cautiously inched away from

the threat of the other. Inch by inch, they edged. Inch by inch, Coyote came closer to the door. Inch by inch, and now he was there. He burst from the house and bolted away.

"I'll never again eat with a snake!" he gasped as he ran.

"I'll never again eat with a coyote!" said the snake, gulping the rest of his rat.

As Coyote was running, he knew—yes, once again he knew—he was hungry. He stopped and sat and howled with hunger, and knew all the time that he—clever Coyote—had run away from a feast! He howled and howled, and then he went on, searching for something to eat.

COYOTE MARRIES THE WHIRLWIND

Coyote went on. He came to a place where a single tipi stood. In front of this tipi boiled a pot of tongue and another one of soup. A girl was standing there, so Coyote went over to talk with her.

"How did you come here?" asked the girl.

"I am traveling and camping out," replied Coyote. "This I like to do."

"You like to camp?"

"Yes."

"Ah!" said the girl, looking him up and down. "You are welcome here. Are you hungry?"

"Yes!" said Coyote. "I'm always hungry."

The girl gave him some tongue and some soup.

"This is very good," said Coyote. "Your husband must be fat from such good food!"

"I'm not married," said the girl.

"What's this?" said Coyote. "How does that happen?"

"No one will marry me because I move camp so often," said the girl. "Do you want some more food?"

Over his newly filled bowl, Coyote said, "What is the matter with these men? It is pleasant to camp at evening where the flowers smell sweet and the grass is green."

"This is how I think also," said the girl.

"I love to camp among the flowers. It is healthier to camp always in a new place." Coyote ate and ate. The food was so good that he had a thought. "Perhaps we should marry, for we think much the same way."

"That's a good idea," said the girl.

On the night of their wedding, the girl prepared a feast with many kinds of food.

"This is the life!" said Coyote as he ate.

The next morning the girl prepared a large breakfast.

"This is the life!" said Coyote, barely able to walk because he had eaten so much.

"We are going to move camp!" said the girl.

"Very well," said Coyote, all the while thinking he would rather take a nap. They took the tipi down and put everything between the travois poles. The girl turned her face to the south, the west, the north, and the east, and called her dogs: "Come on! We are going to move!" The dogs came and were hitched to the travois. Coyote and his wife began to move camp.

And such a moving!

When Coyote looked aside at his wife, she had turned into a great whirlwind. The first thing he knew, he was up in the air. Sometimes he fell on his back upon the sharp cactus, and sometimes the wind whipped him over a log, so rapidly did they move! All his clothes were torn, and his hair

was tumbled about. She tossed him into the air and down to the ground. She dragged him through mud and water until he was nearly dead. Just as he was completely exhausted, she stopped.

"We'll camp here!" she said. She took the pack from the dogs and turned them loose to the south, the west, the north, and the east. "Go now! I'll call you again when I need you."

Coyote lay on his face, gasping for breath, as she put up the tipi and unpacked the pack.

"What are you doing?" his wife scolded. "You told me you loved to camp! Better get up and get some water."

Coyote got up, took a small bucket, and drew water. When he returned to camp, supper was ready.

"Yes, indeed!" Coyote said, looking at the food. "This is what I like! I love to camp!"

"Good!" said his wife. "Tomorrow we'll move again."

Another moving day and I'll surely die, Coyote thought as he ate.

After supper he walked out alone to smoke

his pipe. What am I going to do? he said to himself. Because tomorrow I'll surely die!

Just then Groundhog came up. Coyote told him his troubles.

"If you've married Whirlwind, there's not much I can do for you," said Groundhog.

Coyote's weariness overcame him, and he howled with sadness.

"I have an idea," said Groundhog. "I can't promise anything, but—"

"Tell me!" said Coyote.

Groundhog dug a hole deep into the ground. "Go there," he said to Coyote. "And stay there for four years."

"Go under the ground?" said Coyote. "And stay there for four years? I'd rather die!"

"Have it your way," said Groundhog.

"Very well," sighed Coyote. He started down the hole.

Soon Whirlwind came out to see where Coyote had gone.

"Where is he?" she asked Groundhog.

Groundhog sat on the hole so Whirlwind couldn't see it. "He's gone," he said.

"Well," said Whirlwind, "if he isn't back in four years, I'm not going to look for him anymore!"

"That's only fair," said Groundhog.

Whirlwind went back to her tipi, and Groundhog went off.

Coyote went on under the ground for four years and explored the worlds down there. When he came out, he went on—*slowly.*

Coyote took his tales, some from here and some from there, some about him and some about them, and some about strange and mysterious things.

Coyote went on.

He still goes on, because Coyote is one of the Old Ones.

NOTES ON SOURCES

At first, the stories weren't written down. They were passed orally from person to person. A succession of storytellers picked and chose bits and pieces of what they heard and combined the motifs to tell their own stories. Around crackling winter fires, the storytellers laughed and paused and glanced around, rose and spoke and played a role, and the stories spread as far and as fast as there were people to tell them and people to hear.

Most of the stories in this collection are Coyote stories. The trickster Coyote appears in tales from many Native American cultures, especially those of the Great Plains, the Plateau, and California. Some of these stories are not Coyote stories. They come from areas in which Coyote himself does not appear in tales. Coyote, of course, is one of the Old Ones and knows all the tales.

All the stories are based on material gathered firsthand from Native Americans by anthropologists, ethnologists, and others who study folklore. The materials were sometimes recorded in the form of mere notes. I have taken the liberty of the storyteller in the selecting of motifs and in the focusing of each story, but I have not done so thoughtlessly. Stith Thompson's *Tales of the North American Indians* has been a particularly valuable guide, but I am indebted to many other people as well—a long list of knowledgeable writers and generous tellers.

MONSTER ROLLING SKULL

Dismemberment is a widespread motif in Native American stories. The head usually has the power to move around by itself, and does so in tales from the central and eastern Woodland culture areas, as well as those of the Great Plains, the Plateau, the Northwest Coast, and California. The remaining elements of "Monster Rolling Skull"—Coyote's trickery of the people and the thwarting of his trick—are also well known. This particular version of the story is based on an Alsea tale recorded by Leo Frachtenberg in *Bulletin 67* (1920) of the Bureau of American Ethnology. The Alsea tribe once lived in western Oregon and on its Pacific coast.

HOW THE INDIANS GOT CORN

Corn was an important food in most Indian cultures, and stories of its origin are ubiquitous. This version is based on an Abnaki tale recorded by Mrs. Wallace Brown in the *Journal of American Folk-Lore,* 3 (1890). The Abnaki people are from Maine, New Hampshire, and Vermont.

I have placed within this tale a poem from the Southwest. "The Corn Grows Up" is reprinted from Washington Matthews' Navajo "Songs of Sequence," *Journal of American Folk-Lore,* 7 (1894).

THE SKELETON MAN AND THE MEDICINE OF BLOODY HAND

Both tales are based on material from the Seneca recorded by Jeremiah Curtin and J. N. B. Hewitt in the 32nd *Annual Report* of the Bureau of American Ethnology (1918). The Seneca tribe, from the woodlands of New York, Pennsylvania, and Ohio, is a part of the famous League of Five Nations.

THE WARRING HANDS

The trickster's buttocks talk to him, and so do other parts of his body. One tale, known everywhere but along the Pacific

Coast, finds the trickster—under various names—hoodwinking some dancing birds that he hopes to eat. Sometimes the talking body parts are helpful and sometimes they are contentious. The motif of warring hands comes from Paul Radin's "From the Winnebago Trickster Cycle," *Memoir* #1 of the Indiana University Publications in Anthropology and Linguistics (1948). The rest of the story is pure Coyote, developed from his character as shown in stories of many other food-gathering attempts.

COYOTE FREES THE BUFFALO

This story is based on a Comanche tale recorded by H. H. St. Clair in the *Journal of American Folk-Lore,* 22 (1909). Members of the Comanche tribe of the southern Plains—New Mexico, Colorado, Kansas, and southward—were among the first horsemen of the Plains.

THE MAIDEN'S PROMISE

This story is based on an Okanagon tale recorded by James A. Teit in the *Memoirs of the American Folk-Lore Society,* 11 (1917). The Okanagon peoples' homeland was in northern Montana and Idaho, and reached into Canada.

THE FEAST THAT WASN'T

Based on material in Mathilde Cox Stevenson's 11th *Annual Report* of the Bureau of American Ethnology (1894), this is a tale from the Sia, a people of the southwestern deserts and mesa lands.

COYOTE MARRIES THE WHIRLWIND

This tale is based on a Mandan–Hidatsa tale reported by Martha Warren Beckwith in *Memoirs of the American Folk-Lore Society,* 32 (1938). The two farming tribes—Mandan and Hidatsa—shared similar social structures. They lived mostly in North Dakota, but were also known in South Dakota and Minnesota.